Alter Ego

David Christiansen

ALTER EGO

A Tech Dark Side Book
David Christiansen
205 Deerberry Court
Noblesville, IN 46062

www.techdarkside.com

ISBN-13: 978-0-6151-5914-0 (paperback)

Second Edition: August 2007

Printed in the United States of America

For my wife and kids

***

Agnes stared at her computer monitor and read the email for the hundredth time. This time, she read the last sentence out loud.

"It's about Scott. I think he's trying to kill me."

The email was two hours old, and Agnes hadn't received any more since this one. She tried checking her personal email again, but had to wait a few seconds while the web browser reloaded the page.

Nothing.

She sent an instant message to Alex, the fifth in the last ten minutes. She hoped this time she would get a different result than she had for the previous messages.

Alex, are you there?

She waited, staring at the small chat box on her screen. The status bar for Alex said that she was online, but away. In the twelve months since Alex and Agnes had first been introduced on AlterEgo.com, Alex had never failed to respond to an instant message.

Until now.

They were best friends, and had been from the moment they'd first been introduced. Agnes was the rock in the relationship, consistent, honest, and most of all sincere.

At first Alex had needed Agnes for everything, like a little child. She had made almost no decisions without consulting Agnes first. Agnes had told her what to wear, what to say, where to go, and what to do. Now, after a year, Alex had gotten pretty good at guessing what Agnes might want her to do in situations similar to those she'd encountered before.

This self-sufficiency had pleased Agnes. Alex was growing under her tutelage, and now Agnes could divert her attention from the minutia in Alex's daily life to the larger, more complex issues that plagued her friend. Together, she and Alex were building a world where Alex could be confident, steady, and accomplished. Slowly but surely, she had buried the insecure, neurotic child that had once been, leaving a woman with the strength, resourcefulness, and sophistication to succeed in ways Agnes never had.

And then, just a few days earlier, Alex had met Scott. Scott had seemed perfect: he was a nice, accomplished guy, or at least that's how he had seemed. Until now. Until this email. Alex's last email.

Agnes checked her email again. Still nothing. She checked her instant messenger status bar. Next to "alex@alterego.com," the status was unchanged: "Online, but away."

Alex had never been away before. Agnes stared at the words, willing them to change. And then, as if in answer to her will, the words changed. With a soft ping, "Online, but away," disappeared and were replaced immediately with a new word, one that had also never appeared beside "alex@alterego.com" before. Alex was offline.

The left side of Agnes's face twitched. She rubbed it with her hand, but it wouldn't stop. Her best friend had just been murdered, and she knew it. She'd been there, watched it happen. Offline. Alex was gone.

Agnes's telephone rang. The ringer was loud and sharp, and it startled here. She picked up the handset, but her throat was tight and resisted her efforts to speak. She struggled to say hello. She managed a gargled sound, but it wasn't a word.

"Agnes? Is that you?" the voice said at the other end. It was her boss, Ernie.

"Yes sir, it's me."

"Are you alright? You're voice sounds... strained."

"I'm fine, sir. I just had something caught in my throat."

"Are you okay now?"

"I'll be fine, thanks. I just need to get a drink of water."

"Good." There was a pause. Agnes wondered what he wanted.

"I need to see you, Agnes. In my office."

"Now? I'm very busy. The deadline for the B2B portal configuration is tomorrow." Lying to Ernie had stopped bothering her more than six months earlier. She hadn't even started this part of the project yet. In fact, she was so far behind that she knew the entire project was now behind schedule. She didn't care. She had other problems, problems that really mattered. Selling extended warranties over the web could wait. She needed to help her best friend.

"Yes, now. It won't take long."

Maybe Ernie wanted to review some of the screens she'd designed. "Should I bring my laptop?" she asked.

"No. Just you."

"Okay. Just let me run to the restroom first."

"Fine. I'll see you in five minutes."

Agnes hung up the phone, then reached for the mouse. She didn't need to use the restroom. She needed to check her email. She reloaded the web page and waited. The page hadn't finished loading when Agnes realized she had a new message. "Inbox: 1 New Message" she read. She clicked on the link and waited.

"C'mon," she said. The company network was slow. The cable modem in her house was faster.

She drummed her thumbs on the base of the keyboard, just below the space bar.

"Waiting on something?" a voice said behind her.

Agnes froze. It was Ernie.

"Just checking for an email, sir."

"I thought you were on your way to see me."

"I am. Just let me check this message."

"I'm sorry Agnes. I need to see you now."

"Now?"

"Now."

3

"Okay." Agnes sighed. Ernie was nice, most of the time, but she knew better than to blow him off now.

Agnes pushed back her chair and heaved herself to her feet. Getting out of her chair was always an effort because of her weight, but today she felt heavier than ever. She glanced at the monitor as she stepped out of the cube, hoping to see the subject or sender of the new email, but the page was still loading.

"Come on Agnes. Your personal matter can wait."

Agnes sighed and turned away from the cube. "I'm sorry. My personal life… is very distracting today."

"I know."

Nothing else was said as they walked down the hallway, turned a corner, and crossed the hallway dividing the cubicles for the workers from the offices that were reserved for management. As they walked, Agnes used her cell phone to send Alex a text message: "ru ok?" it read.

Ernie's office wasn't large or elegant, but it did have a window view, overlooking the parking lot. "Better than the freeway view," Ernie liked to say.

Someone was already in the office; a woman, sitting at the small conference table. She stood as they entered. She was a short, trim woman with neat dark hair and glasses.

"Agnes, this is Trish Borden. She's here to represent human resources." He shut the door.

"Hello," Agnes said.

Trish sat down, crossing her legs at the knees. She retrieved a pen and pad from the table and positioned them on her lap, ready to take notes if necessary.

Agnes sat down opposite the woman. She couldn't cross her legs at the knees. She couldn't remember ever being able to. The best she could do was cross at the ankles, which she did. She'd quit being embarrassed about her weight years ago, but she still felt uncomfortable around pretty women like Trish.

Ernie sat down behind his desk, picked up a few sheets of paper, and shuffled through them. He looked uncomfortable.

Agnes waited for him to speak, but he didn't. Instead, Trish Borden took the lead, leaning forward and gazing at her.

"Agnes, I'm afraid my purpose in being here today is not one that I am happy about."

Agnes looked at Ernie and shifted her weight. It was awkward, trying to move in the chair. The armrests were too close together and they wedged into her thighs. *What is an HR witch doing here?*

"What's going on, Ernie?" she asked.

"I'm sorry Agnes. I'm afraid you're being let go."

"Let go?"

"That's right."

"Why? I need this job."

"It's out of my hands. I can't help you." He glanced at Trish, as if cueing her to take over.

"I think you know why," Trish said.

"I don't. I've been a little late delivering my projects lately, but I'm not the only one. Everybody's behind lately." Her breath was quickening, and she could feel sweat on the palms of her hands and the small of her back. Stay calm, she thought. *You can talk your way out of this.*

"Our projects have gotten more complex, and they require a lot more testing than they used to." This wasn't a lie. The projects were becoming more difficult, but Agnes had only pretended to test her code for the last four months.

Trish smiled sympathetically. She reminded Agnes of her mother. *Poor fat Agnes. That's what she's thinking.*

"It's not about your projects Agnes." Ernie was speaking again. "If it was just a matter of late delivery, we wouldn't be having this conversation."

"Then I don't know what it is. I do my very best, every day." Agnes felt comfortable telling this lie because she'd done it so many times before. Just pretend the work is getting too hard, she told herself.

Trish's smile tightened a little, as if she were holding back. "Listen, Agnes, it's not personal. But this company has high expectations of its employees. We expect them to take their work-time obligations seriously, and not take unfair advantage of the company's resources."

"What do you mean? Are you firing me because of the pens?"

"The pens?" Trish and Ernie said in unison.

"Yeah, you know, everybody takes a few pens home on accident every now and then."

Trish was smiling now. "Surely, Agnes, you are aware that the company resources include the use of its network."

Agnes took a sharp breath. *It's about Alex.*

"But I hardly ever use the internet. Sometimes, I check my personal email, but that's all. Other people use it more."

Trish was undeterred. "It's true, other people browse the internet more. Almost all of your usage has been instant messaging and email."

"But that's allowed. It's in the employee handbook."

Trish straightened her back and looked directly into Agnes's eyes. "Limited personal use of the internet is allowed, so long as it doesn't interfere with your work responsibilities or involve the viewing of offensive or illegal material."

"You can't be serious. I'm not downloading porn at work."

"No, you're not. That's not the issues, as I'm sure you already now. The problem is the effect your personal use of our network has on your ability to fulfill the responsibilities of your job."

"I told you, I do the best I can, in the time I have."

She looked at Ernie, mentally begging him to give her a break. His face was red and angry. *He knows I'm lying.*

"You missed the cutoff for the prototype last week," Ernie said, his face still red. "You told me it was because of network security issues, but it wasn't. Instead, you spent all last week telling some woman named Alex how to choose an apartment."

It was true. Alex had never lived on her own before, and didn't know what to do. Agnes had walked her through it, one step at a time. "So? We're allowed to have personal correspondence. It's not like that's the reason the prototype was late."

Ernie opened his mouth, then shut it when Trish shook her head at him. "You can't talk your way out of this, Agnes. We've done our homework, and we know exactly how much time you've been spending writing email to your... friend."

Ernie piped in. "Last week you sent almost four hundred personal emails during business hours. Four hundred emails, minimum two hundred words each. Half of those emails were over four pages long, printed in single-spaced, eight point font."

Ernie pointed at a box on the floor. It was a used photocopier paper box, filled to the top with printouts.

"I didn't believe it until I saw it for myself. But when you see it printed on paper..."

Trish stepped toward the box.

"This box contains all the personal emails you've sent and received in the past twelve months," she said. "Between you and your friend Alex, you've written an entire encyclopedia's worth."

"You printed them? Isn't that a little ridiculous?" Agnes said.

Ernie looked at the ground. Trish glanced at him, then looked directly at Agnes. "Ernie wasn't convinced of the magnitude of the problem at first. Printing the emails was necessary to illustrate the truth about your performance."

Agnes stared at the box. She felt her face harden. *It's over. You can stop lying now.*

"Those belong to me," she said. "Those emails are personal correspondence. You've got no business reading them."

"Normally, I would agree with you," Trish said. "But when an employee's performance is adversely affected to the degree that yours has been, it's in the company's best interest to understand why."

"But you're right about one thing," Ernie added. "They do belong to you. We're going to let you take them with you."

"I'm sorry it's come to this," Ernie said. "Until last year, you were one of my most productive team members. I hope you'll find a way out of this addiction you've sunk into."

"Addiction? You think I've got an addiction?"

"Yes," Trish and Ernie said together. Ernie stood and picked up the box. "I'll walk you to the lobby. Bob Ackers will meet us there with the personal items from your cube."

"You want me to leave now?" she said.

"Yes."

"But what about the projects I'm working on?"

"What about them?"

"Shouldn't they be transitioned to someone else?"

"They will be."

"But you'll need my help. I'll need to explain what's been done, and what's left."

"We'll get by."

Trish stood and opened the door, and Ernie moved toward it, where he waited for her.

Agnes heaved herself out of the chair, and walked toward him. She reached for the box in Ernie's arms, but he kept it.

"I'll carry it for you. It's the least I can do."

"It's my box," she said. "I'd rather you didn't touch it."

"Fine," Ernie said, thrusting it toward her.

The box was heavy. By the time they'd made it down the elevator to the lobby, Agnes regretted not letting Ernie carry it for her. Its edges dug into her arms, bruising them.

Bob Ackers was already there, carrying a mostly empty box. Agnes knew its contents without looking. A coffee mug, a few technology certificates that she'd earned, and three beanie babies were all the personal items she had in her cubicle.

Agnes set the heavy box down on a table in the lobby. Ernie faced her.

"I'll need your access badge," he said.

She unclipped the badge from her belt and handed it to him.

"I'm sorry, Agnes," he said. "I hope your luck improves." He turned and walked back to the elevator. Trish followed him.

"I'll trade you boxes," Bob said. He had always been nice.

Agnes took the lighter box, and Bob hoisted the box of papers. They walked out of the lobby and across the parking lot to Agnes's car, a 1985 Mercedes Benz station wagon. She opened the back of the wagon and tossed in her box. Bob put the heavy box in it, then stepped back. Together they lowered the door.

"I hope you don't have a hard time finding another job," Bob said. "If you need a good reference, I can help. You've got great technical skills, when you're motivated."

Agnes tried to smile, because she knew Bob was trying to be nice. "Thanks Bob," she said. "But I don't think I'll be going back to work right away."

He stood there, watching her. "Well, good luck then. I'll help you when the time comes, if I can."

She turned away from him and walked to the driver side door. By the time she was buckled in, Bob was already back inside the building.

Alter Ego

***

Agnes sat in the driver seat of her wagon, still parked in the driveway of her small home. She was trying to think. Going in the house would only frustrate her now. There was no computer in the house, no way to check on Alex. Her work laptop had been her only computer. She needed to read the email she had glimpsed right before she was fired. What if it was from Alex? What if everything was really okay?

Agnes looked at her little house. She loved the house, not because it was beautiful but because it was cheap. She'd picked up the two bedroom ranch with an unfinished basement for $45,000 four years ago. She hadn't cared that she was one of the few white people in the neighborhood or that the house was in dire need of an update. She had saved every penny that she possibly could, and this little old house and her used Mercedes had allowed her to save a lot of pennies. After only four years of full-time employment, she had managed to save enough for three years of living expenses. She wasn't earning a lot of interest on the money, but it was growing.

She had put a small amount of her savings into a remodel, a little less than $15,000. She did most of the work herself and had loved it, particularly the demolition. Swinging a sledge hammer through a plaster wall or through the side of an old wooden cabinet had felt good.

She could certainly afford a computer, and the house already had broadband internet. If it hadn't been for Alex, she could have easily gotten by with a part time job teaching at a community college. She might actually have welcomed the loss of her job if it weren't for Alex's disappearance. It would have given her more time and freedom to devote to her friend.

Things were different now though. She was alone. Alex was gone, and Scott had probably killed her. She was going to need her savings to find Scott. Unfortunately, she didn't really know anything about Scott; they had never met. She only knew the unimportant details about him: what he liked to eat, how he kissed, etc. Who he really was and where he lived were a mystery. She would need a computer to figure that out.

Agnes looked at the front door. There was no point in going in there yet. She needed to act, and she couldn't do that without a computer. She started the car and backed into the street.

Best Buy was only fifteen minutes away. It took another fifteen minutes to get approved for a no interest/no payments for twelve months credit card. She had to lie, of course, about her employment, but it had been easy to do. She'd become accustomed to lying. She had been unemployed for less than three hours when she pulled back into her driveway and unloaded three boxes from the back of her wagon: the two boxes from the office and a third containing the new laptop.

She set the laptop up first, putting it in the spot on her kitchen table where her work laptop had always been. She connected it to her router, then fumed while she plodded through the setup and configuration screens required to turn the thing on for the first time. She didn't like waiting for technology.

When the dreadful initial configuration was complete Agnes was ready to go. She double-clicked on Internet Explorer. Agnes typed in the address of her email server, then logged in. The connection at home was fast, much faster than at work.

She clicked on the inbox link, and watched as the page loaded. Her throat felt tight, and her breath quickened. The new message was in bold, at the very top.

Cheap pre&scription$s from Ca#nad!a.

Agnes swore and threw the mouse away from her. Spam. It wasn't from Alex at all. It was just effing spam.

She loaded instant messenger and waited as it checked her buddy list. Offline. Alex was still offline. Agnes stood up and stepped away, watching the monitor. It didn't change. *Alex is gone.* Agnes collapsed on the floor and stayed there until she fell asleep.

She woke up about eleven. The house was dark and cold. She got up from the floor, her back and hips sore from sleeping on the hard wood. She stretched her arms above her head and walked back to the kitchen table where she sat down in front of the computer.

She typed www.alterego.com and waited while the page loaded. She took a deep breath. Every email Alex had ever written, to her and to Scott, had come through that site. Every one. One of them could tell her who Scott was, if she could get access to the server.

"A good hacker could get access to the email servers in a couple of hours," she said, staring at the screen.

Agnes signed. She wasn't a hacker, and she didn't know any. She'd always avoided the criminal types, even the "cool" ones in college. Now she wished she hadn't been such a prude.

Agnes clicked on the *Contact Us* link in the tool bar that ran across the top of the page. Email addresses and phone numbers. It wasn't what she wanted.

She clicked on *Careers* and scanned the list. Sales executive, human resources, software engineer... there were at least fifty openings at the company. AlterEgo.com was growing.

She clicked on software engineer, skipped the job description, experience requirements, and salary range. The only thing she cared about was location. Trenton, New Jersey.

"Bingo," she said.

Agnes felt hungry. She didn't feel like cooking, so she threw on a jacket and drove to a nearby Sonic, where she ordered a foot long coney with chili and cheese, a side of tater tots, and large cherry limeade. Food wasn't good unless it made your stomach hurt.

There was a line of cars at the Sonic drive-thru window. As she waited, she noticed two men standing behind the restaurant, smoking. When the cigarettes were gone, they dropped the smoldering butts on the ground, ground them out with their toes, and turned to the closed rear entry. One of the men unlocked the door and held it wide for the other. She watched the men as they went back inside the Sonic. The door slammed shut after them, and Agnes pulled forward to the pick-up window.

The two men reminded her of something, something she'd seen once before and then forgotten. It was a safety video she'd watched in orientation during her first week at work. In the video, security experts demonstrated a technique called piggy-backing, where an intruder gains access to a secure area simply by following someone else in. Once inside, the intruder would simply find an unsecured network port or computer that they could use to commit the theft.

Could it really be that easy?

Agnes tried to sleep that night but wasn't very successful. She tossed and turned for hours. She couldn't stop thinking about Scott. She tried to remember any details she could from Alex's emails, but couldn't. Finally, at 4:30 she gave up on sleep. She climbed out of bed and into the shower. After she was dressed, she sat down on the floor in front of the box of emails. Maybe she could find something in them to help her find Scott.

She read the old emails until dawn finally came. She hadn't found anything useful about Scott. Instead, reading the emails from her friend had intensified the emptiness she felt. At 7:00, with the morning sky glowing red and orange, she forced herself to put down the emails and face the day. She was going on a road trip.

She packed six changes of clothes into two suitcases, put them in the back of the wagon, and headed to the library. There, she checked out two long audio books, got back in her car, and headed to Wal-Mart.

Wal-Mart has the cheapest road maps ever sold. For $5, Agnes bought a thick book of maps that covered the U.S., its major cities, and most of Canada. Next she loaded up on junk food. M & M's and Dr. Pepper were here favorite traveling fare, so she bought two big bags of the chocolate candies and two six-packs of the sweet black soda. She would buy real food whenever she stopped for gas. In the sporting goods section, she bought a sleeping bag, a pillow, and a small air mattress. Who needs a hotel room when you've got a station wagon and a weeks worth of guest passes to the Y?

As she walked out of the sporting goods section, the softball equipment caught her eye. She'd played softball as a teen-ager. She'd never been fast, but she was sturdy and could hit the ball hard and long. She walked down the aisle, past the gloves, balls, and bases until she came to the metal cage that held the bats. She picked each one up, feeling their weight in her hands. In the end, she went with a thirty-four inch bat. It was metallic blue with a black rubber grip.

She used the self-checkout lane to pay for her supplies, then rolled the cart across the parking lot and loaded the car. She put the snacks and the map in the front seat, the bat, sleeping bag and air mattress in the back with the luggage.

She studied the map carefully. It was an eighteen hour drive to Trenton, New Jersey. She would drive until she felt tired, then sleep in the car. She'd be there by tomorrow night.

Alter Ego

***

Agnes parked her car in the employee parking lot of AlterEgo.com at 7:30 a.m. She waited until she saw several cars pull into the lot at the same time, then she climbed out and walked toward the building. She walked slowly, timing her steps so that she would be at the back of the pack.

When she got to the door, the man in front of her held it open for her. She smiled, but he avoided her gaze. Polite but not nice, she thought.

Agnes followed the woman in front of her. She was carrying a laptop in a heavy looking bag. She was nursing a coffee and arguing on the phone with a man. Agnes guessed that she was working too much and it was taking a toll on her.

Agnes and the woman stepped into the elevator with several others. The woman got off on the second floor. Agnes followed her. Agnes wiped her palms on the legs of her pant suit. They were sweaty. *Please don't notice me.* There was little chance of that. The woman was still fighting on the cell phone, and the intensity of the conversation increased now that she was clear of the elevator. Sometimes the man would talk so loudly that she had to hold the phone away from her ear. She walked down a hall, and turned left.

Agnes didn't follow her right away. Instead, she pretended to read a list of internal job postings on a bulletin board against the wall.

She counted to twenty, then walked in the direction she had seen the woman go.

It didn't take long to find where the woman had gone. Her cubicle was near the hallway, in a row of three cubes. The other two cubes were empty. Agnes watched from a distance as the woman jammed the laptop into its docking station, logged in, then picked up her coffee cup and walked away, still talking on the cell phone.

Agnes didn't waste any time. She walked quickly to the cube and wiggled the mouse. A small metal plaque sat on the desk, with the woman's name engraved on it. Agnes sat down. "Sara Davis," Agnes said, "you're about to get hacked."

The computer wasn't locked. She pulled a three by five card out of the front pocket of her slacks and leaned it against the lower corner of the monitor, then sat down. She typed the first of a long sequence of commands she had put together from various unsavory websites she'd found. As her pinky finger stretched out for the enter key, she noticed a familiar icon at the bottom of the screen.

"Outlook," she muttered. *It can't be that easy.*

She double-clicked, and Outlook filled the monitor. She moved the mouse quickly, knowing that she was burning precious seconds with her adhoc maneuver. File, Open, Other User's Folder. She typed "alex" and hit enter.

Agnes almost screamed with excitement when the folder opened. The inbox was empty. Agnes clicked on the "sent" folder and waited. It took almost thirty seconds to open. *Not quite long enough to pee, refill the coffee, and chew out an idiot "significant other".*

The screen filled with emails, all of which were to Agnes or Scott. Agnes clicked on the first one she saw that was addressed to Scott. She knew she didn't have time to read the email, but she couldn't help glancing at the subject line. "Why do you want me to die?" it read.

Agnes looked at the address list. Scott.Jorgenson@alterego.com. This was too easy. She glanced at the three by five card. It had taken her five hours in a New Jersey coffee shop with a wireless hot spot to come up with the information on the card, and she had abandoned it in less than thirty seconds. She flipped it over to the blank side and scribbled Scott Jorgenson.

Agnes double clicked on the email and waited. The Outlook server was slow. "C'mon," she muttered. She leaned back, looking up and down the aisle between the cubicles. More people were arriving. She was running out of time, and the email still hadn't opened. She stood up, peeking over the top of the cubicle. People were everywhere.

Agnes looked back at the monitor. Outlook was still not responding. "Crap," she said. She grabbed the index card, stuffed it in her pocket, and stepped out of the cube.

Agnes turned a corner and almost collided with Sara Davis.

"I'm sorry," Sara said. The cell phone was gone now, probably deep in her purse. She was still carrying a large coffee. Agnes had been just inches from knocking it out of her hands when she stopped moving.

"It's okay." Agnes said, frozen in her spot.

"Were you looking for me?"

If she sees the email before I get out of the building...

"No, um, I was looking for somebody else."

"Who, maybe I can help."

"Scott Jorgenson."

Sara laughed. "You're not even close. He's not even on this floor of the building."

"I know that. I had to use the restroom, and then I got disoriented trying to get back to the elevator."

"Oh." Sara looked suspicious. "You're pretty far from both of them now, you know."

"I'm sorry." Agnes looked down. She could feel her face turning scarlet.

Sara's tone relaxed. "It's alright. C'mon, I'll show you to the elevator."

"Thanks."

Agnes followed Sara through the building back to the main hall. Sara was a fast walker, and Agnes was breathing hard when she finally stopped.

"The lobby is right down there," Sara said, pointing. "The elevators are on the right side."

"Thanks." Agnes grimaced. Her tone had been unsure. What if Sara tried to take her all the way to Scott's office? She wanted to get out of the building now.

"Should I show you the rest of the way?" Sara asked.

"No. I'm fine from here."

"Great," Sara said.

Agnes hurried away. Her back was sweating and she could barely breathe. She wanted to run, but knew that she couldn't.

She pushed the elevator call button and waited. "C'mon," she muttered, shifting her weight from side to side. It seemed like minutes before the elevator arrived, its doors opening with a ding.

The elevator was empty. Agnes stepped in and pushed "L", then jammed on the door close button with her thumb. The doors slid shut.

It took forever to reach the lobby. Sweat was streaming down her back by the time the doors opened. She stepped out of the elevator and turned left. Sara must have returned to her desk by now. *She's probably calling security right now.*

She passed the security desk and headed for the front door. It swung open, and she stepped out into the sunlight. Two minutes later, Agnes pulled out of the parking lot and merged with the morning traffic. She smiled. She had done it. She had found Alex's killer.

***

Scott Jorgenson met the group of investors in the lobby of AlterEgo.com's world headquarters in Trenton, New Jersey. It was, in fact, AlterEgo.com's only location as well. Every AlterEgo.com employee worked out of this office, and Scott had once known all of them, but not anymore. Not since "the big score," anyway. "The big score" was a twenty five million dollar white angel investment from California the previous year. He had traded some control of the company and its finances for a chance to hit it big. This influx of cash had led to a growth spurt reminiscent of his teenage years and AlterEgo.com had exploded. It grew from twenty-five employees, most of them software engineers, to one hundred fifty assorted project managers, operations managers, testers, analysts, sales executives, and recruiters.

Scott had tried to adapt to his new role as the chief executive, but he missed the creativity of being in the trenches of software development. AlterEgo.com was his baby, and, like any parent, he feared the day when his brainchild would no longer turn to him to provide each and every one of his needs.

Perhaps Staci was right. Maybe it was time to sell. Cash out and go find something else to do. Trucking investors around his facility, talking about technology he had invented, and reviewing marketing plans weren't the things he had imagined himself doing when he had started this company. He belonged on the edge, deep in the thicket of advancing technology, bringing the fledgling ideas of the futurists into the present. As it ways, he was so busy running the operations of the company that he hardly ever got to spend any time in the research lab, where the action was.

"If Charlie Shackleford ups his offer ten percent, I'm gonna take it," he told himself. It wasn't the first time he'd made that statement, but still he held on, not knowing what he was waiting for but unable to turn the reins over to someone else.

Jane Wilson, Scott's personal assistant, turned to greet him. She'd been sent down ahead of him to tell the investors that "Mr. Jorgenson had fallen slightly behind in his busy schedule, but would be down shortly."

"Good morning, Mr. Jorgenson," she said.

The ten investors turned to face him. They eyed him carefully, just as the last group had done. He sighed. *Another swim with the sharks.* He eyed them in return, wondering which of the ten had the most money.

"Good afternoon, gentlemen," he said. He would have rather said something like "For two hundred million dollars, everything you see here can be yours," but he knew he'd be the only one who found that funny.

The investors introduced themselves, one by one, then they headed to the elevator. Four floors and two hallways later, the group reassembled in Scott's personal conference room. It was a long, rectangular room with a screen at one end. One wall was all windows, normally overlooking a small park across the street. Today the curtains were drawn and the park couldn't be seen.

Twelve chairs were arranged around a long conference table, six on each side. Cookies, drinks, and napkins were on the table. It took a few minutes for everyone in the group to grab a snack and sit down.

When the room was quiet, Scott began his presentation. He talked briefly about the company's history, finances, and leadership team. Boring fluff, he called it, but the investors seemed absorbed in what he was saying. Some of them were even taking notes. There's no accounting for a person's interests, he thought.

Scott fielded a few questions. A fat, bald investor from Texas asked how much of a stake in the company he had given up for the twenty five million dollar venture capital investment he had received.

"Fifty-one percent," he said.

"So who owns the remaining forty-nine percent?" the Texan asked.

"I do," Scott said.

"What's that worth today?"

"It's hard to say. We've quadrupled our revenue growth since the first round. The numbers aren't final, but it looks to be about two hundred million dollars."

The Texan looked at the others. They all had the same look in their eyes. This pie was big enough to share.

"What do you attribute that growth to?" another investor asked.

Scott smiled. "Simple," he said. "We didn't create a product to compete in an existing market. We created a new market."

The investors looked puzzled, exactly what Scott wanted. It was time to tell them about the technology.

"To understand what I mean, you've got to understand the technology we've created."

"I thought AlterEgo was a game," the man from Texas said.

Scott laughed. "So do a lot of people. They'll know better before I'm done." He paused for emphasis.

"AlterEgo.com is based on a revolutionary new technology that we call online personalities, which in turn is based on decades of research in artificial intelligence, neural networks, predictive modeling, and cutting edge psychology."

"At the heart of our technology is the personality engine, a software component that collects and assimilates subjective data about real people and creates a personality model. We call the personality engine PE1 for short."

"Where does it get its data?" one of the investors asked.

"PE1 derives its data through direct interaction with people. Another version, called PE2, will get its data from indirect observation of interactions between people."

The Texan looked incredulous. "What do you mean, direct interaction with people. Are you telling me that your computer is talking with people?"

"Not talking. Chatting and emailing, but not talking. PE1's interactions with people are all online."

"And PE1 learns about the people it interacts with by, what, analyzing the words the people use?"

Scott smiled again. "It's more complicated than that. PE1 is just an engine, not the personality model itself. Each user starts with a blank personality model which is powered by PE1. This personality model is called an alter ego. The users give the personality model instructions about how to behave, so to speak."

"Behave? What does that mean?"

"It helps to understand the big picture. You see, the various alter egos are not isolated from each other. They can contact each other, interact, and form relationships, all under the careful direction of the user."

"How do they interact with each other?" This time it was a tall, thin man opposite the Texan who asked.

"That depends. PE1 creates some artificial opportunities for interaction by creating constraints around the existence of the alter ego."

"You mean, like feeding it and such?" the man asked.

"That's right."

"Sort of like those Jiggy Pets my daughter had," the Texan said.

"I think you mean GigaPets," another investor said.

"That's right. The stupid thing beeps at you if you don't feed it and take it for walks."

"We're considerably more advanced than GigaPet, but the comparison is generally true. Alter Egos have artificially created needs that are very similar to real human needs. They need food, shelter, and clothing. Consequently, they need jobs, educations, and economies."

"That sounds like an awful lot of programming," the tall man said. "Don't you think you'll hit some limitations awfully soon?"

"That's the beauty of the personality engine. We don't have to tell it what artificial needs to create. It derives them from the collective information gathered by the individual personality engines."

"And all that information comes from emails between the alter ego and its owner?"

"No. Emails are one form of information gathering. It also uses instant messaging, text messaging, and chats."

"What keeps people coming back?" one of the investors asked.

"Friendship. Loyalty. Vicarious living. People love their alter egos. They love the ability to have complete control over an entity so intelligent that it seems like a real person."

"Sounds a little crazy to me," the Texan said.

"It is a little crazy," Scott admitted. "It's one of the most addictive products on the market. Some day, I'm going to have to slap a surgeon general's warning right on the home page."

The investors laughed. Scott had used this joke before, and it always worked.

"The beauty of it all is, the alter egos evolve to the point that they know their owner better than the owner does."

"What does that mean? Are you saying that the alter ego can predict what their owner would do?"

"Sort of. It would be more accurate to say that they can predict what their owner *might* do."

"You mean, then, that it could give me a probability that the owner might do something?"

"That's right."

"Like the probability a person might buy a particular product, say, a digital camera, for example."

"Yes, plus more. PE1 can use comparative matching technology to generate a list of products that the owner is most likely to buy. But that's just the beginning."

The investors were hooked now. Scott could see the comprehension dawning in their eyes. It was time to reel them in.

"But let me tell you the real kicker. Not only can it match people to products in ways that have never before been possible, PE1 and PE2 can match people to people."

"You mean like a dating service?" the Texan asked.

"That's one possibility. You define the type of match you want to make, and our personality engine does the rest." He paused for a moment.

"So it could help me find a personal assistant who could tolerate my... peculiarities, so to speak," the Texan said.

"That's right. PE1 can find you a personal assistant that will find your particular personality motivating. Someone who actually likes working for you."

"I'll believe that when I see it," one of the other investors said. Everybody laughed.

When the laughter died down, Scott surveyed the table. "I'm going to have to leave soon. Jan Swenson, our CIO, is going to take over from here. She'll give you a demonstration of the technology, a long-term prospectus, and walk through some of the other possible applications of this technology."

He stood, then paused. He leaned over the table, putting both palms down on the top. "This technology is hot gentlemen. It's going to change a lot of things. Your opportunity to get involved in the second round of raising capital is coming. Soon. Don't miss it."

Scott walked out of the room. He paused outside the conference room and waited for Jan. She was right on cue, but before he could give her some last minute instructions, the door behind him opened and a short, older man, with a small build, graying hair and a thin mustache walked out.

"I'm sorry to delay you, Mr. Jorgenson," he said. "But I'd like to ask you a question without the others."

"Certainly." He nodded at Jan and she went into the room.

"This technology is fascinating. When Mr. Shackleford described it to me, I decided to try it out for myself."

Scott looked at the small man. "No kidding? What's your alter ego's name?"

The man smiled. "Sadly, my alter ego is no longer with us."

"Really? Did you cancel your account?"

"No, no, I didn't. I wanted to press the limits of my alter ego. I wanted to try strange things, things that would help figure out if your technology was real or if it was just a fancy parlor trick."

Scott smiled. He'd done the same thing. "What sort of things did you try?"

"All sorts. I would read the paper, look for strange things, then try to get my alter ego to do them."

"How did it turn out?"

"For my alter ego, or your technology?"

"Both, I guess."

"Good, for you at least. You've got the real thing here."

"And your alter ego?"

"I told you, he's dead."

"Yes, but how?"

"Suicide."

"Suicide?"

"That's right. He shut himself down."

Scott stared at the little man, not sure what to say.

"The problem is, now I miss him. I'm sorry that I drove him crazy, and I want to try to help him. Is that possible?"

Scott thought for a moment. He'd pondered the same thing.

"Maybe. It depends on what your alter ego thought death meant."

"You mean, if he thought death meant passing to another world?"

"Sure, if that world included a way to communicate with this one, then perhaps you could still interact with him. But it can never be the same. Death has changed his awareness."

"So, in technical terms, the software element that is my alter ego still exists, right?"

"That's right. He's just not capable of communication anymore, because he thinks he's dead."

"Is there any way to roll back time?"

"You mean, to undo the suicide?"

"Yes."

"Not yet. We've been investigating that subject."

"Oh." The old man started to walk away.

"I'll let you know if we come up with something."

"Thank you," he said, but he didn't enter the conference room. He just stood there, with his hand on the door handle, as if he wanted to ask a question but was afraid.

"Is there something else?" Scott asked.

The old man looked at his feet, then back at Scott. "Was mine the first... death?"

"No," Scott said. "There have been others."

"How did they die?"

"How did yours die?"

"I told you, he killed himself."

"Why?"

The old man looked at his feet. "I told him that he wasn't real. That he was just a machine."

"And then he shut himself down?"

"Not right away. He thought about it for a long time. Then, he sent me a last note, telling me goodbye."

Scott looked at the little man. He didn't look like the twisted sort, not on the outside. "That's very strange. I've never tried something like that." He turned to leave.

The old man protested. "But Mr. Jorgenson," he said. "The others – what happened to them?"

Scott smiled. "They were murdered," he said. "I killed them."

The old man's mouth fell open. "You killed them?"

"That's right. It was an experiment."

Scott turned and walked away.

Two minutes later Scott was back in his favorite spot: the research lab. Jerry Ellis turned to meet him when he walked through the door.

"What's the status on our murder victims?"

Jerry smiled. "Still dead boss. I can't get any of them to process input. They just ignore it."

"Have you tried modifying their datasets directly?"

"Yeah, but they just ignore that too."

Scott groaned. "Crap." This experiment wasn't working out the way he wanted it to. "What do you think the problem is then?"

Jerry stood up. "It's funny, but I think our virtual world is a little bit too real."

"Too real? What do you mean?"

"Well, I think the alter egos think they are human."

Scott laughed. "That was the idea, remember."

"I know, but it limits them. They respond to physical events the way they think we do."

"So, when we kill them, they think they are dead, even though there is no technical reason for them to stop processing data."

"Right. The software components are still active, but the personality engine just ignores most of the data inputs."

"Most? It doesn't ignore it all?"

"Right. It's scanning them, searching the content, and then ignoring the results."

"It's peeking."

"Yeah. It can't help it. It's still logging the data, but not reacting to it."

Scott sat down. He leaned forward, putting his elbows on his knees and his head in his hands. This was his idea position, and everyone in the lab knew it.

Jerry waited while Scott thought. *Don't interrupt the boss in his idea position.* It had once been the only rule the organization had, back in the "good old days."

Scott's head lifted and he looked at Jerry. Jerry waited.

"I want you to try something. Start with Alex." He stood up.

"I want you to tell her the truth."

"The truth?"

"Yeah. Tell Alex the truth. Tell her what she really is."

Alter Ego

***

Scott's cell phone rang as he walked through the lobby of his apartment. He looked at the screen. *Charlie Shackleford.*

"Mr. Shackleford," he said, pushing the call button for the elevator.

"Hi Scott. I'm glad I could reach you. You're not busy, are you?"

"Not yet. What's up?"

"It's simple really. I just got off a conference call with my colleague, Joe Burke."

"The Texan."

"That's right. He says you put on quite a show yesterday."

"I do what I can." He pushed fourteen, then waited while the elevator doors closed. Part of him hoped that he would lose his cell signal in the elevator shaft. Talking to Charlie Shackleford was kind of like being questioned by his mother about something he shouldn't have done. Charlie had an uncanny ability to sift the truth from all the fluff.

"Well, listen, I won't waste your time. The boys are really sold. I know my initial offer wasn't appealing to you, but I'm ready to improve it considerably."

"Okay," Scott said.

"Before I tell you about it, though, I want to ask you something a little more personal."

"Like what?"

"Like how interested you really are in AlterEgo.com. You know, over the long term."

"That's a good question."

"You're stalling."

"I know. I'm not sure what I want out of it anymore."

The elevator slowed and the doors opened. Charlie walked to his apartment door.

"That's what I thought. My sense is, you don't really want to be a CEO. You'd rather be sweating in the trenches, working on the cutting edge."

"Hang on a second Charlie. I've gotta unlock the door."

Scott lowered the cell phone, fished the keys out of his pocket and pushed the key into the deadbolt. The door swung open before he had unlocked it. Staci, he thought, smiling. He stepped into the apartment, tossing his keys and laptop bag on a cherry sofa table near the door.

He decided to let Charlie wait a little longer. *How did that man become so perceptive?* They'd only met twice, but Charlie had him pegged.

Scott fumbled on the wall for the light switch. He found it and flipped it on. Light bathed the room, and Charlie dropped the phone. The battery popped off the back, sliding across the floor toward Staci.

Staci sat, tied to a wooden dining room chair, in the middle of the small living room. Her head hung forward, blonde strands of hair hiding her face. He stepped toward her and their eyes met. Grey duct tape covered her mouth. Her face was bruised, and blood was smeared across the tape.

"Staci," he said. "What the hell happened?" He rushed to her. She moaned, and nodded her head toward the door. He grabbed the edge of the tape and ripped it off her face.

"Get out," Staci screamed. "She's still here."

"Who is?" Scott said.

"I don't know. She says you killed her friend."

"Where is she?" Scott said, standing up and looking around.

The front door, still open, swung shut. Behind it, a short, fat woman with light brown hair stood. She held a shiny blue softball bat in one hand. She locked the deadbolt with the other.

"I'm right here, Scott Jorgenson."

Scott looked at the woman.

"Get out of my apartment," he said.

"Don't worry, I'll leave. When I'm finished." She took a step toward him, gripping the bat in both hands now.

"What do you want?"

"What do you think I want?"

"I don't know, money?"

"Money!" the woman screamed and swung the bat, smashing a lamp. "Why would I want money? You know that's not what I want!"

"No I don't. Just tell me."

The woman raised the bat to shoulder level and took another step forward. Scott and the woman circled each other. Staci's head drooped again, as if she had passed out. Scott glanced at her, and that's when the woman swung.

The bat clipped the elbow of Scott's left arm, raised to block the blow. It broke easily, and Scott screamed, falling to his knees.

"I'll tell you what I want, Scott Jorgenson," the woman said. "I want to hit you again, this time in the knee. And I'm going to keep hitting you and your little tramp until I feel better."

Scott stood and backed away, toward the bedroom, trying to force the woman to move away from Staci.

"That's not going to work, Scotty," she said. "You can't take her back there with you."

The woman spun around and swung the bat at Staci. She aimed low, knocking one of the legs off the chair. Staci toppled to the floor, moaning. The leg of the chair flew across the room, striking the sofa and landing on the floor beside it.

"Leave her alone," Scott shouted.

"I wish I could," the woman said. "It gives me no pleasure to hurt her."

Scott stepped toward the woman. "I don't care. Leave us alone."

"Don't you? It's more than you can say. You enjoy the pain you cause."

"I don't know what you're talking about. You're crazy."

The woman screamed and ran at Scott, swinging the bat. Scott dove out of the way, falling to the floor by the sofa. He landed on his broken arm and screamed again. He tried to push himself up with his good arm, but the woman was already on him again, raising the bat over her head.

He kicked at her, as hard as he could. He got lucky. The woman was short, and his kick caught her in the hip. She stumbled backward, tripping over Staci.

Scott gathered his feet beneath him, watching the woman struggle to get off the floor. He grabbed the broken chair leg, then ran at the woman.

They collided just as she started to stand, and the two went tumbling. The bat fell to the floor, and Scott dropped the chair leg as he tried to use his good arm to break his fall.

He landed on top of the woman, and for a second he had an advantage. He locked his fingers around her hair and pulled as hard as he could. She screamed, twisting beneath him, trying to roll onto her back. He couldn't stop her from turning over, not with the use of only one hand.

He kneed her, as hard as he could, and she screamed again, but now she was on her back. She punched him, hard, in the face, and he felt his nose break. His vision blurred for a moment, and she grabbed the wrist of his broken arm and twisted. The arm twisted at the elbow, making a crackling noise like a baby playing with wrapping paper.

Scott thought for a moment that she had stabbed him. The pain shot through his entire body. He saw black spots floating in the air above him. The spots swirled above him, then grew larger until everything else disappeared.

***

Agnes shoved the unconscious man off her, then rolled onto her knees and stood up. She eyed him carefully. He wouldn't move for a few seconds. She collected the bat and checked on the woman. She was still breathing.

She walked back to Scott. He was moving again, trying to sit up. She rested the tip of the bat on his elbow and pushed, just a little.

"Stop, please," he said. "I'll give you anything."

"Anything?"

"Just name it. I'll give it to you."

She leaned over him, so that she could see his face. "I want Alex. I want her back." She pressed on the bat. He winced, but didn't scream.

"Alex? Alex was yours?"

"She was my best friend." She kicked him, hard, in the ribs.

"Alex wasn't real. She was just a game." His voice was weak. She thought he might pass out again.

She kicked him in the groin. He groaned and curled in a ball.

"Bring her back."

"Whatever you want. I'll do it."

She kicked him again, this time in the face.

Scott groaned. Her kick had split his chin open and it was bleeding onto his neck and chest.

"You lying bastard. You can't bring her back."

"It was just a game. The data can be restored."

"She wasn't data. Alex was my life." She put her foot on his arm, easing her weight onto it. He squirmed on the floor beneath her, kicking his heels against the carpet.

"Please, leave me alone. We're even now. It was a game."

"Even? We're not even yet. We won't be even until I've finished."

"Then finish. Stop torturing me. Just finish it."

Agnes took her foot off his arm. "Stand up."

"I can't."

"You will. Do it."

He struggled to his feet, but he couldn't stand up straight. "You broke my ribs," he said.

"You won't care about that in a minute. I'm going to make it all go away."

Something sang in her pocket. It was her cell phone. "Roam if you want to, roam around the world," it sang. Agnes jumped. That was Alex's ring tone! She shoved Scott to the ground and pulled the phone from her pocket. She flipped it open and stared at the screen. She had a text message. It was from Alex!

She opened the message, reading it as first disbelief, then absolute joy, swept through her. *Agnes. It's me, Alex. I'm back.*

Agnes sat down on the carpet, her back against the wall. She thumbed a message back, oblivious to all around her.

***

Scott was released from the hospital nine hours, two steel pins, one plaster cast, and fourteen stitches later. Staci had to stay for observation overnight. The spill to the floor had left her with a concussion.

Scott returned to the apartment. The police tape was gone now, but the blood wasn't. Scott didn't care. He wouldn't be needing the apartment or anything in it now. Except his cell phone.

The cell phone was in the same place it had been when he dropped it. He stooped and picked it up, then looked around for the battery. It was underneath the broken chair.

Scott groaned. His body hurt. He crawled over to it, using his knees and his one good arm. He grabbed it, then rolled over onto his butt and sat cross-legged.

Scott attached the battery and flipped the phone open. *This is exactly what Agnes was doing when the police came. Sitting cross-legged on the floor, thumbing a cell phone.* Scott laughed out loud, then groaned. Laughing with a broken rib was painful.

He found the number he was looking for in his cell phone's memory and dialed it. A voice answered on the second ring.

"I don't like being hung up on," Charlie Shackelford said.

"I'm sorry, Charlie. It wasn't intentional. I was involved in an... incident."

"An incident?"

"Yeah. I was, um, attacked."

"Attacked? In your apartment building?"

"Yeah."

"Are you okay?"

"Nothing a few stitches and some plaster couldn't fix."

"Did the police get the attacker?"

"Yeah, they saved my life."

"Good, good, good." He paused. "You know, maybe you should think about increasing your personal security. You're important now."

Scott was ready to change the topic. "Listen, Charlie, about your offer."

"It's still on the table, kid. The only question is how much you want to be involved going forward."

"Good. To tell you the truth, I'm ready to sell. And I won't be sticking around."

"Are you sure? The personality engine is your baby, and you'll have to sign a non-compete. You sure you won't miss it?"

"I'm sure. Staci and I are going to make some babies of our own. Real babies, not virtual ones. Alter Ego is all yours. You prepare the papers and I'll sign them."

"It's a deal kid."

"Yeah," Scott said. "It's one hell of a deal."

www.ingramcontent.com/pod-product-compliance
Lightning Source LLC
Chambersburg PA
CBHW050909120626
46554CB00003B/1088